...Stargazing Tip...

KU-347-670

Give your eyes time to adjust to the dark. You'll see many more stars after 20 minutes of stargazing than you will at the start.

Begin stargazing by looking for a constellation that's in your sky all year round, such as Ursa Major if you're in the northern hemisphere or Crux if in the southern.

The Earth is always spinning, so the stars appear to move across the sky. Pick a constellation and watch it change position after a few hours of stargazing.

If you can't remember some of the constellation patterns, use your imagination to draw your own around the stars.

POWYS POWMAC			
57218000112979			
J520	Dec-2021		

Guinea Pigs
Go Stargazing

Kate Sheehy

If you are like Bob and Ginger and would love to plan a stargazing trip,
please ask an a_____to never, ever
look di_____r eyes.

Powys

57218 00011297 9

Bob and Ginger have always had a
fascination with the night sky.

Every night they would
gaze at the stars through
their bedroom window
with curiosity.

One night Bob asked Ginger,
"What exactly is a star?"

"I'm not sure,"
replied Ginger.

So Bob and Ginger
decided to find out!

They set to work the very
next day. They went to the
library and spent hours
reading books
about astronomy.

Astronomy is the study of the **Sun**, the **Moon, stars**, **planets**,
comets, and everything else in **the Universe**.

"Ginger, look! I found out what a star is!" Bob shouted with excitement.

"A star is a huge spinning ball of hot, glowing gas.

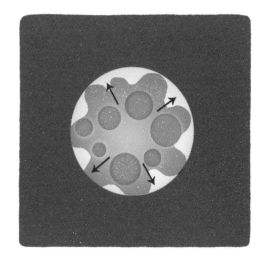

The centre of the star is especially hot and produces lots of energy.

This energy eventually travels out of the star and is given off as heat and light.

That's what gives a star its glow!" He concluded.

"**Guess what else?**" asked Bob. "**Stars are round, not pointy. Our eyes play tricks on us. And they don't really twinkle either,**" he continued.

"**Starlight bends as it travels through a layer of gases called the Earth's atmosphere. This makes a star look like it's twinkling,**" Bob explained.

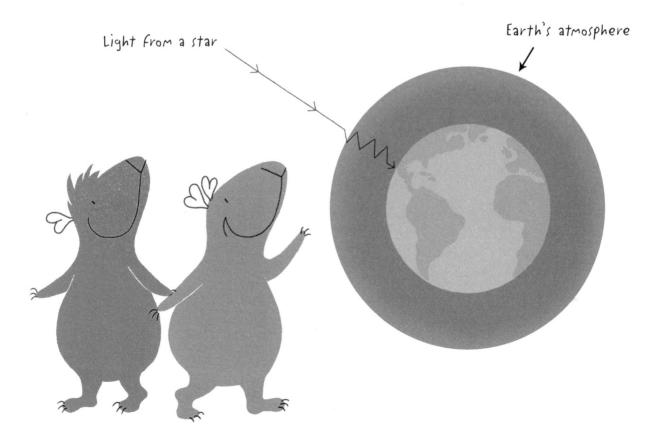

Light from a star

Earth's atmosphere

Stars might appear similar in the sky but they differ in...

size...   brightness...

... temperature, and colour.

All stars are hot, but the hottest are blue and the coolest are red.

The Sun is the closest star to Earth. This yellow dwarf star is average in size and temperature compared to other stars.

Proxima Centauri is the closest star to the Sun. It would take thousands and thousands of years to fly there.

Proxima Centauri is a red dwarf star. It is much smaller and cooler than the Sun.

Rigel is a type of star called a "blue supergiant". Rigel is enormous compared to the Sun and is much hotter.

Bob and Ginger read about imaginary patterns drawn by linking bright stars together. These are called constellations. **"There are 88 constellations in the sky around the Earth,"** cheered Ginger. **"They are in the shape of animals, mythical creatures, people, and objects."**

Leo the lion

Centaurus the centaur

Cassiopeia, queen of the night sky

Lyra the harp

Early stargazers gave the constellations names and told stories about them. **"Would you like to hear the story of Orion and Scorpius?"** asked Bob. **"Yes, please,"** replied Ginger.

"Orion was a fearless hunter who vowed to kill every animal on Earth. This angered Mother Earth so she sent Scorpius, a giant scorpion, to kill Orion.

The God Zeus placed Orion and Scorpius in different parts of the sky.

Orion is in the sky for part of the year until Scorpius comes and chases him away."

"Wow. Great story," said Ginger.

Next, Ginger discovered that the Earth is divided into two halves by an imaginary line called the Equator. **"These halves are called hemispheres,"** said Ginger. **"People in the Northern Hemisphere see different constellations to people in the Southern Hemisphere."**

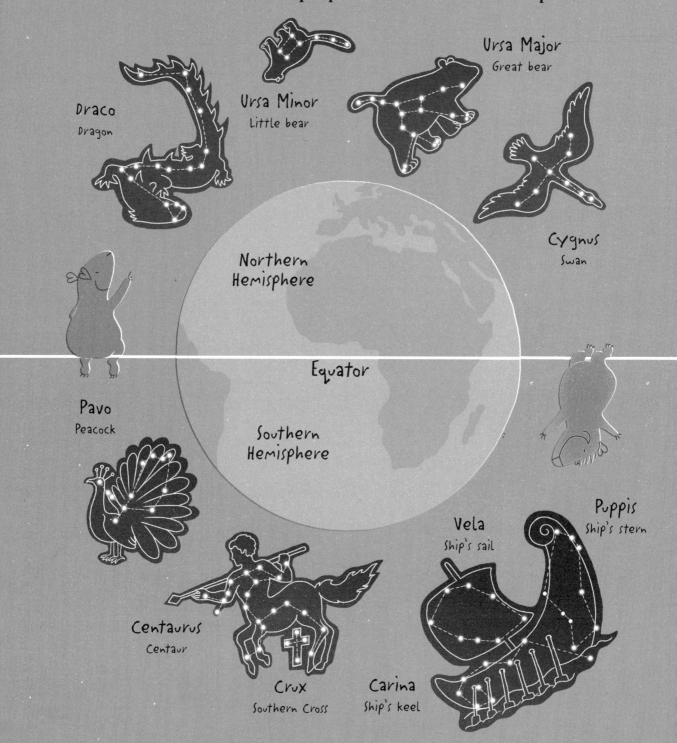

Draco
Dragon

Ursa Minor
Little bear

Ursa Major
Great bear

Cygnus
Swan

Northern Hemisphere

Equator

Southern Hemisphere

Pavo
Peacock

Centaurus
Centaur

Crux
Southern Cross

Carina
Ship's keel

Vela
Ship's sail

Puppis
Ship's stern

"But what about the zodiac constellations?" interrupted Bob.

"They can be seen from both hemispheres!" answered Ginger.

The 12 zodiac constellations form a cirle around the Earth and the Sun.

They form the starry backdrop to the planets and the Moon.

Bob and Ginger were fascinated by shooting stars and wanted to learn about them. **"I would love to see a shooting star so that I can make a wish!"** Bob exclaimed.

Small pieces of space rock called meteoroids come close to Earth.

Meteoroids

Some meteoroids enter the Earth's atmosphere.

Earth's atmosphere

"Bob, did you know that shooting stars are not really stars?" said Ginger.

"Wow, really? What are they?" Bob asked.

Ginger drew some diagrams to help her explain...

what are shooting stars?

Meteoroids fall through the atmosphere at high speed.

They heat up as they rub against the air and become meteors — glowing streaks of light.

The meteors last for less than a second before burning out.

"That is what we see as shooting stars," concluded Ginger. **"Amazing!"** said Bob.

Bob and Ginger were amazed by what they had read but they really wanted to discover space in real life.

Bob had an idea. **"Let's go stargazing and see the stars for ourselves!"** he suggested.

"That's a fantastic idea!" squealed Ginger. They rushed home to gather what was needed for a night of camping under the stars.

Bob found an old telescope in the attic. **"This will do perfectly,"** he said.
Ginger found a torch and a compass.
"These will help us find our way," she smiled.

Map

Compass

Telescope

Head torches

Telescope tripod

They also packed a tent to sleep in. **"Let's bring marshmallows to toast on a fire,"** said Bob.

"And a flask of hot chocolate to keep us warm," added Ginger.

Camping mats

Flask

Sleeping bags

With their bags packed, Bob and Ginger set off. "We will need to go **far away** so that the city lights won't block our view of the stars," advised Bob.

Ginger spotted a hilltop on their map that would make the perfect viewing point. **"We will need to walk across the park and through the forest to get to it,"** she said.

It was beginning to get dark. Bob noticed a bright light shining next to the Moon.

"Ginger, look! I can see the planet **Venus**," said Bob. **"Wow,"** replied Ginger. "It is also called the Morning and Evening Star," she added, "because it can only be seen for a short time before sunrise or after sunset."

Bob and Ginger made it into the
forest, but they were having
trouble finding a way out.

"I can't see a thing through all
of these trees," sighed Ginger.

Just then, Ginger remembered that she had a torch and compass. **"We need to head north,"** said Bob. Ginger held the compass flat and when its arrow pointed north, she shouted, **"Come on, Bob. This way!"**

"There's the hilltop!" cheered Ginger.
"At last," said Bob with a sigh of relief.

It was a tough climb but the view
was worth the wait. Bob and Ginger
could see the Milky Way
shimmering in the dark night sky.

"**Wow,**" gasped Ginger.
"How **amazing** is this
galaxy that we live in?"

"Did you know that
stargazers used to think it
looked like spilled milk?
That's how the **Milky
Way** got its name,"
giggled Bob.

Bob and Ginger began pitching their tent.

Pitching a tent in
the dark, however, was
not an easy task.

Luckily, they had packed
head torches.

Finally, the tent was up
and they were ready to
explore the night sky.

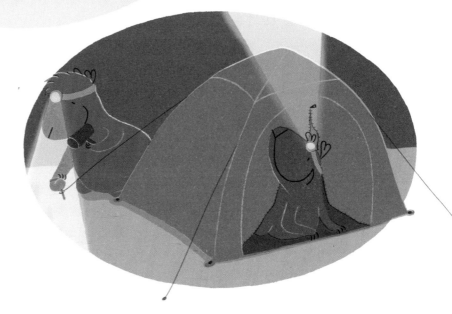

Bob and Ginger used their telescope to see objects in space in more detail.
They saw...

Craters

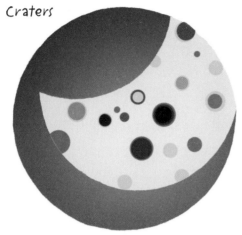

The Moon is covered in craters. They were created by huge space rocks crashing into the Moon.

Hercules globular cluster

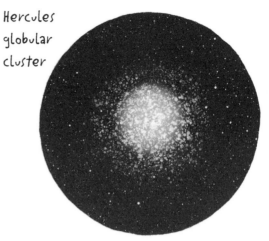

A globular cluster is a ball-shaped group of old stars packed together.

Whirlpool galaxy

A galaxy is a huge group of stars and their planets held together by gravity.

Crab nebula

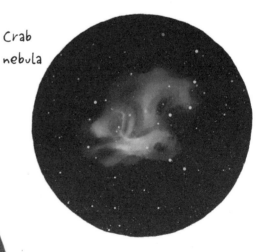

A nebula is a big cloud of gas and dust in space.

Using their eyes,
Bob and Ginger spotted
some constellations.

"There's Ursa Major," said Ginger, beaming.
"I see Ursa Minor, too," said Bob.

"Look! Over there!" Bob shouted.
**"It's Orion and his dog, Canis Major. It looks like they
are going to fight Taurus the bull."**

The night was nearly over. Bob and Ginger had spotted so much but they were disappointed that they never got to see a shooting star.

Bob and Ginger were just about to go to bed when, out of
nowhere, a bright, beautiful shooting star appeared.
"Quick, Bob, make a wish," whispered Ginger.

Bob and Ginger closed their eyes and made a wish.

"Bob, what did you wish for?" asked Ginger.

"If I tell you then it won't come true!" replied Bob.

After a long day and night learning all about stars,

Bob and Ginger cosied up beside a warm campfire.

"What a **magical** evening this was," said Ginger.

"We'll remember it **forever,**" added Bob.

The two guinea pigs couldn't wait for their next stargazing adventure.

Project Editor Amy Braddon
Project Art Editor Victoria Palastanga
Consultant Carole Stott
Editor Sally Beets
Designer Eleanor Bates
Production Editor Abi Maxwell
Production Controller Isabell Schart
Jacket Co-ordinator Issy Walsh
Managing Editor Laura Gilbert
Publishing Manager Francesca Young
Publishing Director Sarah Larter

First published in Great Britain in 2021 by
Dorling Kindersley Limited
One Embassy Gardens, 8 Viaduct Gardens,
London, SW11 7AY

Imported into the EEA by Dorling Kindersley Verlag GmbH.
Arnulfstr. 124, 80636 Munich, Germany

Copyright © 2021 Dorling Kindersley Limited
A Penguin Random House Company
10 9 8 7 6 5 4 3 2 1
001–324558–Oct/2021

All rights reserved.
No part of this publication may be reproduced, stored in or
introduced into a retrieval system, or transmitted, in any form,
or by any means (electronic, mechanical, photocopying,
recording, or otherwise), without the prior written permission
of the copyright owner.

A CIP catalogue record for this book
is available from the British Library.
ISBN: 978-0-2415-1061-2

Printed and bound in China

For the curious
www.dk.com

Seasonal Stargazing

Each year, as Earth travels around the Sun, our seasons change. When we go from summer to winter, we look at different directions in space. This means that different constellations can be seen at different times of year.

Winter in the northern hemisphere

Taurus
Bull

Pegasus
Flying horse

Gemini
Twins

Orion
Hunter

Cetus
Whale

Canis Minor
Little dog

Canis Major
Big dog

Orion
Hunter

Summer in the southern hemisphere